P9-BZM-235

Actual Fairy Size

By Andrea Posner-Sanchez
Illustrated by the Disney Storybook Artists

Random House 🏠 New York

Copyright © 2007 Disney Enterprises, Inc. All rights reserved. Published in the
United States by Random House Children's Books, a division of Random House, Inc.,
New York, and in Canada by Random House of Canada Limited, Toronto,
in conjunction with Disney Enterprises, Inc. RANDOM HOUSE and colophon
are registered trademarks of Random House, Inc.
ISBN: 978-0-7364-2495-0
www.randomhouse.com/kids/disney
MANUFACTURED IN CHINA   10 9 8 7 6 5 4 3 2 1

Welcome to Pixie Hollow, home of Tinker Bell and the rest of the Never fairies. Here you'll find all the comforts of home—beautiful rooms, fancy furniture, and stylish clothes—but perhaps not exactly the way you're used to seeing them.

After all, the fairies are only about five inches tall. So everything in Pixie Hollow is scaled down to their size. And items that serve one purpose for you might be used in a completely different way by the fairies.

For example, think about a thimble, which you use when sewing. To a fairy, that thimble would be the perfect-sized bucket for carrying water from a stream.

actual thimble size: ¾ inch high

5"

*N*ow take a look at your toothbrush. It fits comfortably in your hand and you use it to keep your teeth sparkly white, right? Well, if you were fairy-sized, you'd use it very differently!

When the fairies found a Clumsy's toothbrush (Clumsies are what the fairies call humans) floating in the stream, they came up with some new uses for the strange item.

actual
toothbrush
size:
7½ inches long

9

8

7

6

5

4

3

2

Lily, a garden-talent fairy, tried it out as a scarecrow. Since the toothbrush is taller than any fairy in Pixie Hollow, it would definitely scare flower-eating birds away from her garden!

Beck, an animal-talent fairy, decided it was great for brushing the tails of her squirrel friends. The squirrels certainly liked it!

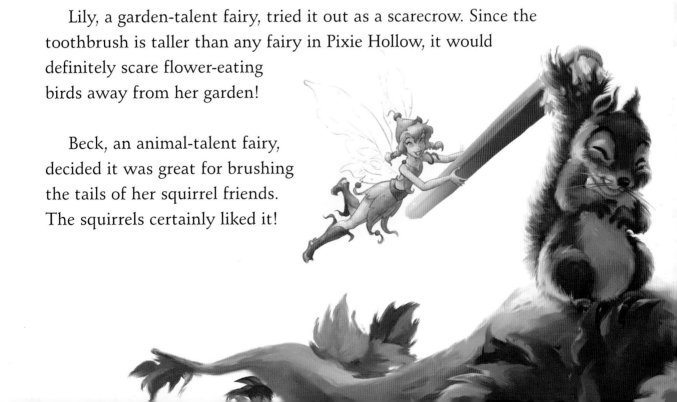

The fairies are great at turning just about any Clumsy item into something practical.

Tink crafted this dagger out of a piece of a pirate's toothpick.

Lily thinks this horseshoe makes a wonderful addition to her garden gate. If the horseshoe is that big compared to Lily, just imagine her reaction to seeing the horse!

actual toothpick size: *2⅜ inches long*

1   2   3   4   5   6   7

The sewing-talent fairies use a peanut as a dress model. Their designs always fit the fairies perfectly.

Think about how many peanuts you can hold in your hand—practically a whole fairy wardrobe could fit there!

Bitty Buildings

A fairy wouldn't be comfortable in our human-sized homes. Just imagine what a hard time a five-inch-tall fairy would have opening doors, getting snacks from the refrigerator, or even sleeping in your bed! Instead, the fairies live in fairy-sized rooms with fairy-sized furniture.

Just about all of the Never fairies live together in a tree. The Home Tree is a towering maple, about the size of those you'd see in your backyard or nearby park. But while you might find a squirrel or a bird family living in those trees, this one is home to hundreds of fairies! All of their tiny bedrooms, plus common areas such as a kitchen and library, are carved into the tree's trunk and branches.

The tiny fairies can fit comfortably inside many things we use every day.

Tinker Bell made her workshop from a Clumsy teakettle that washed up on the shores of Never Land.

actual teakettle size: **10** *inches high*

5"

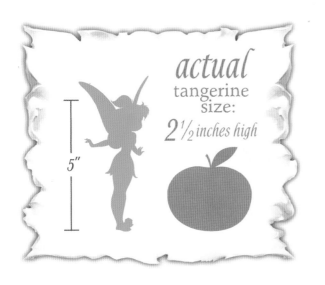

actual
tangerine
size:
2½ *inches high*

5"

Bess likes to have peace and quiet when working on her paintings, so this art-talent fairy found a Clumsy tangerine crate and moved it to a secluded area of Pixie Hollow. Her one-of-a-kind art studio still smells a little citrusy.

If a fairy visited you, where would you have her sleep? Perhaps inside a slipper, on a soap dish, or on a pot holder?

*W*hen you're done eating a peach, you probably toss the pit away. Well, the fairies don't like anything to go to waste. Instead of using stones or bricks, they actually built a mill out of peach pits!

The dust mill, located on the banks of Havendish Stream, is where the dust-talent fairies busily sort Mother Dove's old feathers and then grind them into fairy dust.

About 400 peach pits were used to build the fairies' mill. How many do you think you'd need to build something a human could fit into?

actual
peach pit
size:
1 inch long

1   2   3   4   5   6   7

$\mathcal{T}$hinking of redecorating? Perhaps you can borrow some ideas from the fairies.

Rani is a water-talent fairy, so she loves anything that reminds her of water. Her bed is made of driftwood. Her curtains are made of seaweed. Her floor is paved with river stones. And she has an elaborate armchair made from a seashell.

To relax, try swaying to and fro in a spiderweb hammock.

Or take a long soak in a coconut-shell bathtub.

actual strawberry size: **2** inches high

5"

Big Meals

Take a peek inside the fairies' kitchen and you'll notice that the biggest things in there are the fruits and vegetables. That's because the fairies grow and eat the same produce we do.

Just one strawberry
can make enough yummy
tarts to feed twenty fairies!

Have you ever gone skiing?
Carrying skis is as tough for a human
as toting around string beans is for a fairy!

Preparing meals for all the fairies is a big job, so having a
big work space is important. The large worktable (large to
a fairy, that is) was carved from a piece of driftwood found on the shore.

actual
worktable
size:
15 *inches long*

| | | | | | | |
|9|10|11|12|13|14|15|

Petite Posies

Flowers are lovely to look at, delightful to smell, and fun to make posy chains with. Wait until you see what the Never fairies do with their beautiful blooms!

Queen Clarion's gorgeous gown is made almost entirely of flower petals. The bodice is a velvety red rose. The tiered skirt is made of champagne-colored rose petals. And poinsettia petals were used to create the train.

A fairy flower parasol is practical and fashionable!

Music-talent fairies play happy tunes on their flower trumpets.

*I*nstead of carpets or rugs, the fairies cover the floor of their beautiful tearoom with flower petals. Fresh flowers are brought in every day to keep the room smelling—and looking—fresh.

It takes about twenty-five daisies to cover the floor from wall to wall. Just eight sunflowers will work, too.

Reading lamps in the Home Tree library are made of fluted flowers and lit by trained glowworms.

Orange-blossom petals are used as fairy washcloths. No need for sweet-smelling soaps—the fragrance is built right in!

Tiny Leaves

Leaves come in all shapes and sizes. And the fairies make good use of just about all of them.

The pages in all fairy books and journals are pressed leaves.

Pretty table linens are made from leaves dyed with berry juice and beet juice to turn them a variety of colors.

Berry juice is also used as ink. One blackberry would provide enough ink to write this whole book—if it was fairy-sized!

Other fairies may have fancier outfits, but Tink prefers her simple green leaf dress.

Next time you see a leaf floating down a stream, take a good look—a fairy might be riding on top. Leaves make great fairy boats!

So do turtles!

Wee Critters

In Pixie Hollow, you won't find any oxen pulling plows or horses pulling carriages. But you will discover many small animals (which, of course, aren't small compared to the fairies!) doing big things. You'll be so impressed with what these little animals can do, you may be tempted to teach your pet hamster some new skills!

Fairies love fresh fruits and vegetables such as berries and mushrooms. Preparing the fields, harvesting the crops, and delivering everything to the Home Tree's kitchen is hard work—especially since all the fruits and vegetables are human-sized! Luckily, there are field mice and snails to help pull heavy wagons and farming equipment.

Specially trained fireflies
keep Pixie Hollow lit at night.

Ever since Rani
lost her wings, Brother Dove
has acted as her personal airplane!
Rani rides in feathery comfort on the
broad back of her friend all around Never Land.

Caterpillars are a great source of wool.
When the caterpillars get overgrown and super-fuzzy,
they happily let caterpillar-shearing-talent fairies
give them haircuts. The weaver-talent fairies
can make six comfy fairy sweaters
from the wool of just one caterpillar!

Cricket-whistling-talent
fairies conduct a chorus of
crickets. The crickets love
chirping along whenever the
music-talent fairies perform.

actual cricket size: *1 inch long*

7 6 5 4 3 2 1

Great Games

The fairies love to play games. But don't expect to see them playing with the same sports equipment you have!

On Great Games Day, the fairies compete in a variety of events, including the potato heft, the carrot toss, and the leapfrog race.

Leapfrog is much more exciting when you're riding on the back of an actual frog!

Who needs dumbbells when you're a fairy—potatoes are just as challenging to lift!

actual
carrot size:
from 4 to 7 inches long

5"

When tossed properly, a carrot sails through the air just as well as any javelin!

*W*ant to see how the Never fairies would fit into your world? Carefully remove the attached bookmark from the back of the book. It's a few inches longer than a fairy, so it can also be used as a ruler to help you judge how a fairy would measure up to your hair accessories or favorite toys, for example. And you can imagine new and exciting ways that the fairies would use your things. If you're feeling inspired, try designing some fairy-sized outfits and vehicles. After all, you never know when a fairy may visit you from Pixie Hollow!